Carlos & Carmen

The One-Tire House

books

fragile

más libros

by Kirsten McDonald
illustrated by Erika Meza

Calico Kid

An Imprint of Magic Wagon
abdopublishing.com

For Daydee and Pop—who gave me a typewriter instead of a pony —KKM

To my two Carlos, and specially both of my parents; who taught me to value changes, movings, carnes asadas, mischiefs, surprises and the beautiful moments you can only live with your family. Gracias: ¡los quiero! —EM

abdopublishing.com

Published by Magic Wagon, a division of ABDO, PO Box 398166, Minneapolis, Minnesota 55439. Copyright © 2016 by Abdo Consulting Group, Inc. International copyrights reserved in all countries. No part of this book may be reproduced in any form without written permission from the publisher. Calico Kid™ is a trademark and logo of Magic Wagon.

Printed in the United States of America, North Mankato, Minnesota.
102015
012016

THIS BOOK CONTAINS
RECYCLED MATERIALS

Written by Kirsten McDonald
Illustrated by Erika Meza
Edited by Heidi M.D. Elston
Designed by Candice Keimig

Library of Congress Cataloging-in-Publication Data

McDonald, Kirsten, author.
  The one-tire house / by Kirsten McDonald ; illustrated by Erika Meza.
    pages cm. -- (Carlos & Carmen)
  Summary: The Garcia family is moving to a new house, and twins Carlos and Carmen do not want to leave their small, familiar home--especially since they do not understand why their father describes the new place as a one-tire house.
  ISBN 978-1-62402-140-4
1. Moving, Household--Juvenile fiction. 2. Hispanic American families--Juvenile fiction. 3. Twins--Juvenile fiction. 4. Brothers and sisters--Juvenile fiction. [1. Moving, Household--Fiction. 2. Twins--Fiction. 3. Brothers and sisters--Fiction. 4. Family life--Fiction. 5. Hispanic Americans--Fiction.] I. Meza, Erika, illustrator. II. Title.
  PZ7.1.M4344On 2016
  [E]--dc23
                            2015026224

Table of Contents

Chapter 1
Big Red News

Carlos and Carmen ran into the kitchen. The twins could smell the tortillas warming in the oven.

They could smell the spicy shredded beef they both loved. Most of all, they could smell excitement.

"Your Mamá and I have some big news," said Papá when they sat down to eat.

"Are we getting a new baby?" asked Carlos.

"No, but we are getting something nuevo," answered Papá.

"Are we getting a new puppy?" asked Carmen.

"Definitely no," said Mamá.

Mamá and Papá gave the twins some clues. Mamá said it was big and red. Papá said it had a tire.

Carlos scratched his head and thought really hard. Then he asked, "Is it a big, red car?"

"No," said Mamá. "It is not a big, red car. It is bigger than that."

Carmen scrunched up her face and thought really, really hard. "Is it a big, red monster truck?" she asked.

Papá laughed. "No," he said. "It is not a big, red monster truck. It is bigger than that."

Carmen looked at Carlos.

Carlos looked at Carmen.

"We give up," they said.

So, Mamá and Papá said together, "We are getting a new house!"

"It is big and red," said Mamá.

"And, it only has one tire," added Papá with a big smile and a wink.

Chapter 2
Brushing Up

Later that night, Carlos and Carmen were in the bathroom. They were getting ready for bed.

Carlos was brushing his teeth.

Carmen was brushing her hair.

"I do not want a new house,"
Carmen said sadly.

Carlos nodded his head. His
toothbrush went up and down, up
and down.

"I like this casa best," said Carmen.

Carlos nodded his head again. His toothbrush went back and forth, back and forth.

Carmen said, "I like los patos on the wallpaper in this bathroom. I like our bedroom with the big tree outside. I like the hall closet with the best hide-and-seek hiding place. I do not want to move."

"Ah gah wah ta mo eeda,"
said Carlos with his mouth full of
toothpaste bubbles.

And because they were twins,
Carmen knew her brother meant, "I
don't want to move either."

"Besides," said Carmen, "whoever
heard of a casa with one tire!"

Carmen put her brush in the
drawer.

Carlos spat the toothpaste bubbles into the sink. He turned to Carmen with a foamy toothpaste beard.

"Maybe it's a trailer or a camper with only one wheel left," he said.

"Ooh, yuck!" said Carmen. "Now I really don't want to move."

Chapter 3
Saying Good-Bye

Several days later, Papá brought four big boxes to Carlos and Carmen's room.

"You can finish packing your toys and clothes in these," he said.

"Do we have to move?" Carmen whined.

"Yes," said Papá, "but I think you will like the new, red house. It is bigger. You will each have a bedroom. And, of course, the house has a tire."

"How can a house have only one tire?" asked Carlos as he thought of trailers and campers.

"Just wait, and you'll see," laughed Papá. "And, while you wait, you can pack your boxes."

Carlos and Carmen spent the rest of the day getting ready to move. They packed their shoes. They packed their clothes. They packed their books and games and toys.

Then together they walked around the house saying good-bye to their favorite places.

"Adiós, yellow ducks," said Carlos to the ducks on the wallpaper in the bathroom.

"Adiós, best hide-and-seek hiding place," Carmen said to the empty spot at the bottom of the hall closet.

They went into the bedroom they shared. They walked to the window.

"Adiós, big, old tree," said Carmen, looking out their bedroom window.

"Adiós, little backyard," they said together in sad, quiet voices.

Chapter 4
A House with a Tire

The next morning, Tío Alex came with a big truck. Mamá and Papá and Tío Alex put all of the big boxes inside the truck.

Carlos and Carmen put all of the small boxes inside the truck. They all worked together to put the tables and chairs and beds inside the truck.

When the truck was full, the house was empty. Then Tío Alex and Papá drove off in the truck. Mamá and Carlos and Carmen followed in the car.

They drove across town. Carlos and Carmen looked out of their windows

hoping to see a red house. They saw white houses. They saw green houses. They saw gray houses. Finally, the car and truck stopped in front of a big, red house.

"Let's go see your new rooms," Mamá said with a big smile.

Carlos and Carmen went with Mamá into the big, red house. They walked up the stairs to the second floor.

"This is tu dormitorio, Carmen," said Mamá, opening the door to a yellow bedroom. "And, tu dormitorio is right next door, Carlos."

The rooms were big. They were bright. And, they each had a window that looked out on a tree in the big backyard. Carmen and Carlos gave each other big smiles.

Maybe moving wasn't going to be so bad after all.

Just then, Papá arrived with a big box for Carmen's room. "Time to start unpacking," Papá told Carmen.

"Okay," said Carmen. "But I'm confused."

"Me too," said Carlos. "This house is big and red, but it does not have any tires."

"Oh, no?" teased Papá with a big smile. "Take a closer look at the big tree in your new backyard."

The twins rushed to Carmen's window. They looked at their new backyard. They looked at the big tree.

Hanging from a large branch was a rope. At the bottom of the rope was a tire that was just right for swinging.

In no time at all, the twins were outside.

"You know what?" asked Carmen as she jumped onto the tire swing.

"I think I'm going to like this one-tire house after all."

"Me too," said Carlos, and he gave his sister and the tire a push that sent them sailing up into the sky above their new backyard.

Spanish to English

adiós – good-bye

casa – house

los patos – the ducks

Mamá – Mommy

nuevo – new

Papá – Daddy

Tío – Uncle

tu dormitorio – your bedroom